TiBURÓN

LET'S TAKE CARE OF THE SEA !

ILLUSTRATED BY

ADRIÁN BONNETTE

THIS BOOK BELONGS TO:

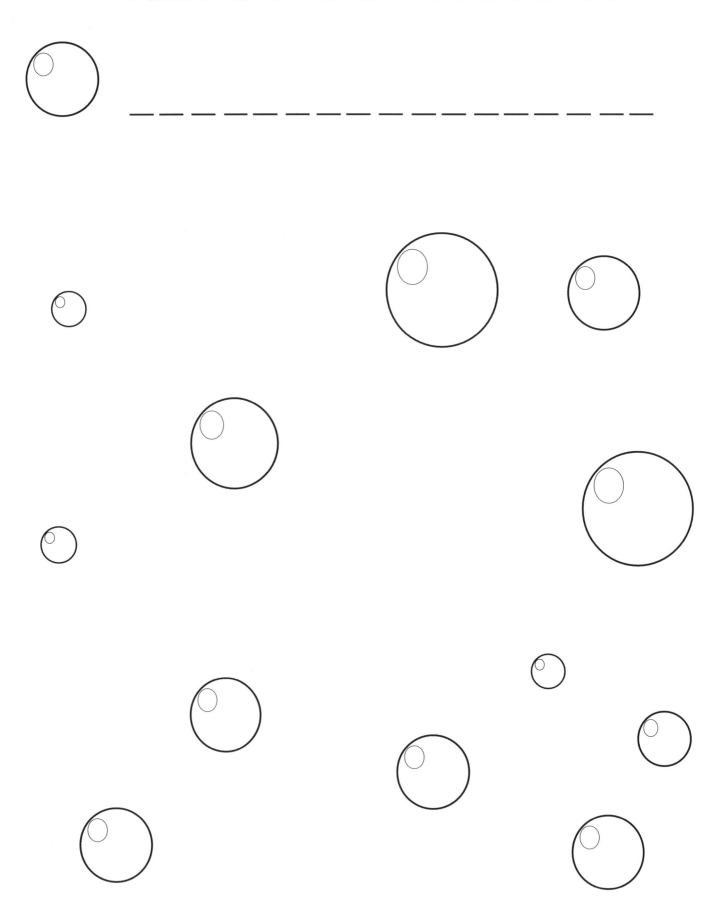

_____

PAINT THE OBJECTS THAT BELONG TO THE SEA

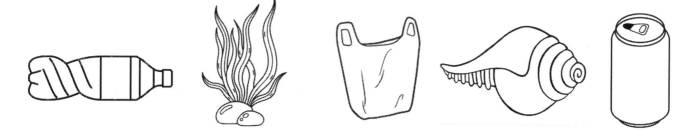

OCTOPUS

S STARFISH

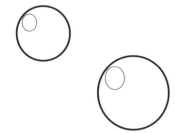

LET'S NOT THROW GARBAGE INTO THE SEA, BECAUSE IT HARMS ANIMALS

TIBURONCY AND LEO THE OCTOPUS, HELPED THE TURTLE TO FREE ITSELF, WELL DONE!!

C CRAB

M MANTA RAY

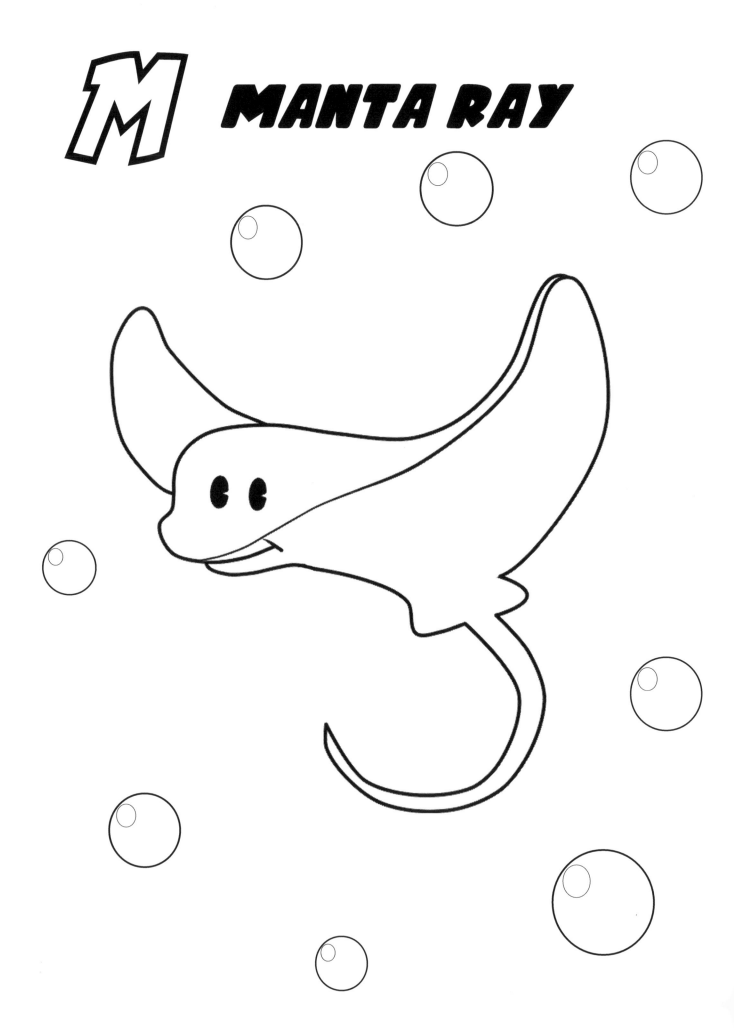

S SWORDFISH

W WHALE

D DOLPHIN

S SNAKE

S SEA HORSE

F FISH

J JELLYFISH

LET'S TAKE CARE OF THE SEA, WITHOUT THROWING GARBAGE IN IT

FOLLOW THE DOTTED LINE

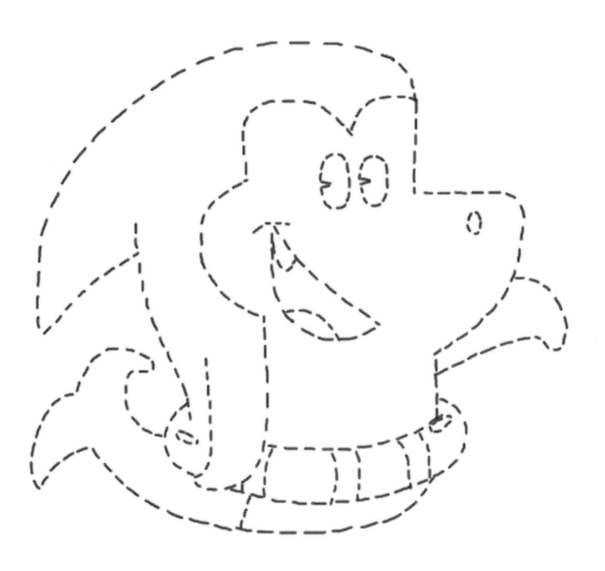

FOLLOW THE DOTTED LINE

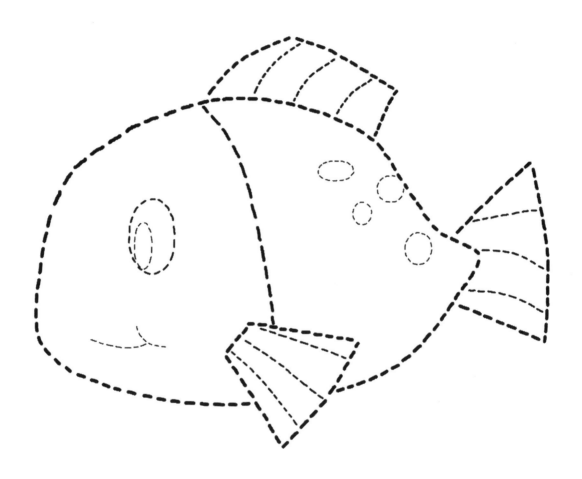

FOLLOW THE DOTTED LINE

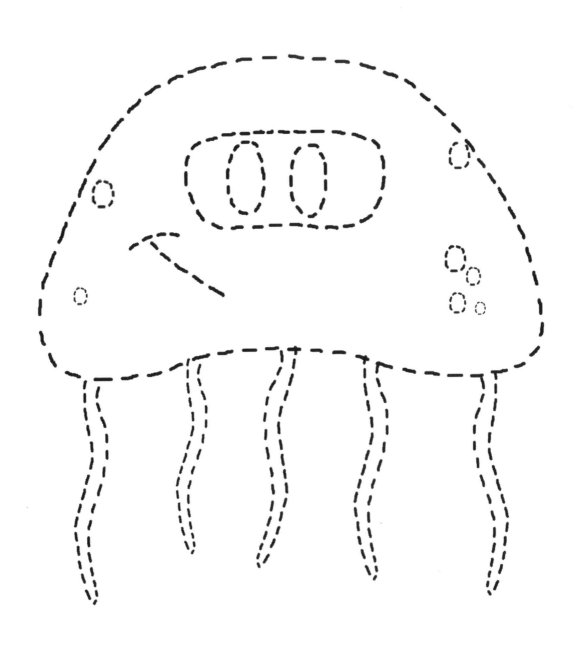

MARK THE SILHOUETTE THAT CORRESPONDS TO EACH CHARACTER

HELP TIBURONCY MEET HIS FRIENDS

Made in United States
Orlando, FL
21 November 2024

54241981R00015